Snuffy Goes to School

Based on a teleplay *Snuffy's First Day of School* by Eleanor Burian-Mohr
and story-edited by John Semper, Jr.

www.tommynelson.com

A Division of Thomas Nelson, Inc.
www.ThomasNelson.com

Published in Nashville, Tennessee, by Tommy Nelson®,
a Division of Thomas Nelson, Inc.

Text: Based on the television series produced by
PorchLight Entertainment, Inc. and Modern Cartoons, LTD.
Characters created by David and Deborah Michel.

One warm and breezy afternoon, Snuffy flew high above Tarrytown with his friends Jay Jay and Tracy.

"Are you ready, Snuffy?" Jay Jay asked. "Are you ready for your first day of school tomorrow?"

"Oh, nooooo!" Snuffy cried. "Why did you remind me?"

Snuffy's wings started shaking.

"What's the matter?" asked Jay Jay.

"I'm afraid of going to school!" answered Snuffy.

"Everyone is a little scared the first day," Jay Jay said.

"I was a little scared," added Tracy. "And so was Jay Jay."

"But I'm a LOT scared!" Snuffy explained. "What if I don't know anybody?

And what if the teacher doesn't like me?"

"Hold on before you blow a gasket," said Jay Jay. "School is full of new friends."
"We promise," Tracy said. "And of course your teacher will like you." But as they
flew home, Snuffy still felt the same way—a LOT scared.

Late that night, while Jay Jay and Tracy dreamed quietly in the hangar, Snuffy rolled around wide awake.

"I don't know what to do," Snuffy whispered softly. Finally, he closed his eyes to pray.

"Dear God, I need help with tomorrow, because I'm afraid about my first day at school. Amen."

When morning's light streamed into the hangar, Jay Jay and Tracy yawned and wing-waggled themselves awake.

"Hey, Snuffy," Jay Jay called. "Time to rise and shine! It's your big day!"

"Time for school!" said Tracy.

They looked left and right.

They looked up and down.

They called, "Snuffy, come out, come out, wherever you are!"

"H-h-hey, everybody," sputtered Herky. "What's up?"

"We can't find Snuffy!" Jay Jay answered.

"And it's almost time for school!" exclaimed Tracy.

"Snuuuuuufffffy!" they yelled, looking for their friend everywhere.

The little planes and the helicopter buzzed all over town in their search.

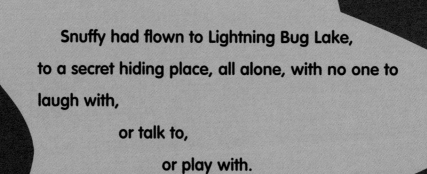

Snuffy had flown to Lightning Bug Lake, to a secret hiding place, all alone, with no one to laugh with,

or talk to,

or play with.

All alone, Snuffy sniffled. "This is no fun at all," he said.

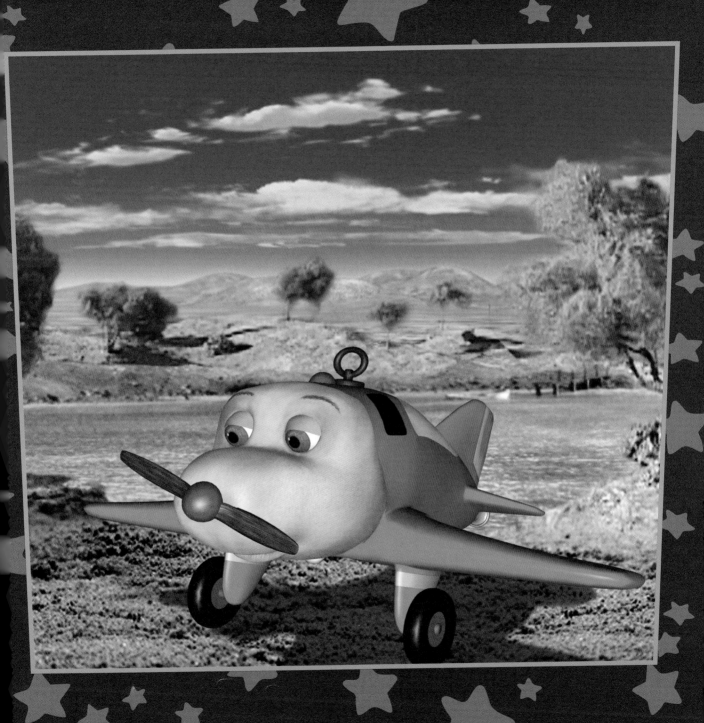

Jay Jay, Tracy, and Herky could not find Snuffy anywhere, so they asked Old Oscar for help.

"Snuffy is scared about his first day of school," Jay Jay explained.

"And now h-h-he's missing," Herky said.

Old Oscar chuckled. "I have an idea," he said. "You three wait right here."

Old Oscar started his engines, taxied outside, and took off.

Old Oscar felt sure he could find Snuffy.

Without looking left and right,

without looking up and down,

Old Oscar flew straight

to Lightning Bug Lake.

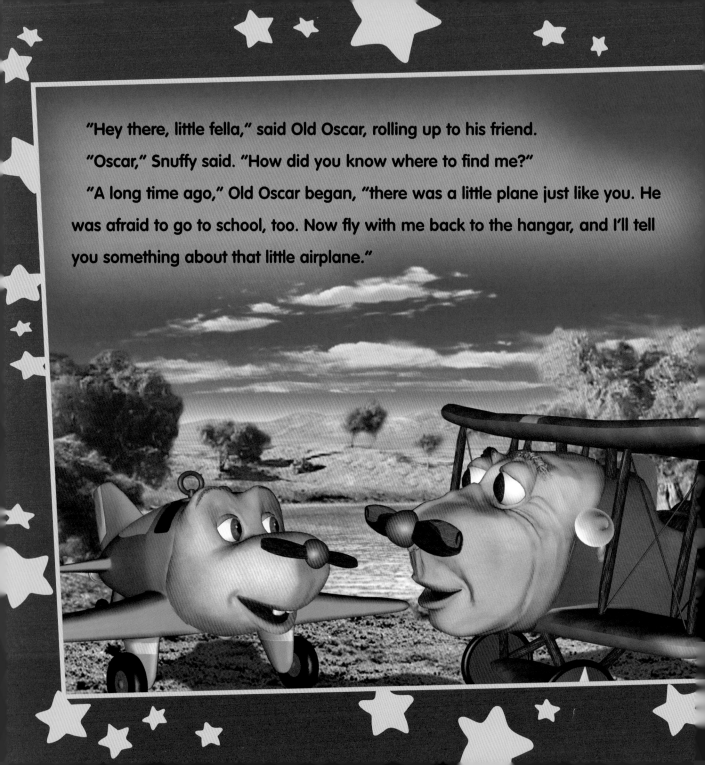

"Hey there, little fella," said Old Oscar, rolling up to his friend.

"Oscar," Snuffy said. "How did you know where to find me?"

"A long time ago," Old Oscar began, "there was a little plane just like you. He was afraid to go to school, too. Now fly with me back to the hangar, and I'll tell you something about that little airplane."

So Snuffy followed his friend into the clouds.

"Yes, sirree," Old Oscar continued, "when that little plane woke up on his first morning of school, he high-tailed it for a hiding place."

Snuffy sniffed. "Who was that little plane?" asked Snuffy.

"Me," answered Old Oscar.

"Really?" Snuffy asked.

"Cross my prop and hope to fly. And just like someone helped me, I'm here to help you. Snuffy, God is always with you. Even at school. Trust Him and you won't be afraid."

Old Oscar and Snuffy landed on the runway.

"I'll let Jay Jay and Tracy take you to school," said Old Oscar. "I have to go now."

"But wait," Snuffy said. "What if I don't know anybody?"

"You'll make friends," Old Oscar answered.

"But what if the teacher doesn't like me?" Snuffy called.

"Trust God to take care of you," said Old Oscar. "That teacher of yours is sure to take you under his wing!"

"We're glad you're back," said Jay Jay. "Are you okay?"

"I'm still scared," said Snuffy, "but I'm going to trust God."

"You'll see soon," Tracy said. "School is so much fun!"

Snuffy turned on his wheels and raced
toward the runway. "Come on!" he hollered.
His friends hurried to catch up.

"Now I'm ready!" Snuffy yelled. "I'm ready for my first day of school! Let's go!" And they all flew into town as fast as Snuffy could fly.

"H-h-here we are," said Herky as they landed by the school.

"Looks like your teacher's waiting for you," said Tracy.

"Where?" asked Snuffy.

"Right there," said Tracy.

"Where?" Snuffy asked again.

Old Oscar taxied over, smiling as big as the Tarrytown sky.

"Well, hello there, youngster," he said to Snuffy. "Now you'd better
hurry—you're almost late for class."

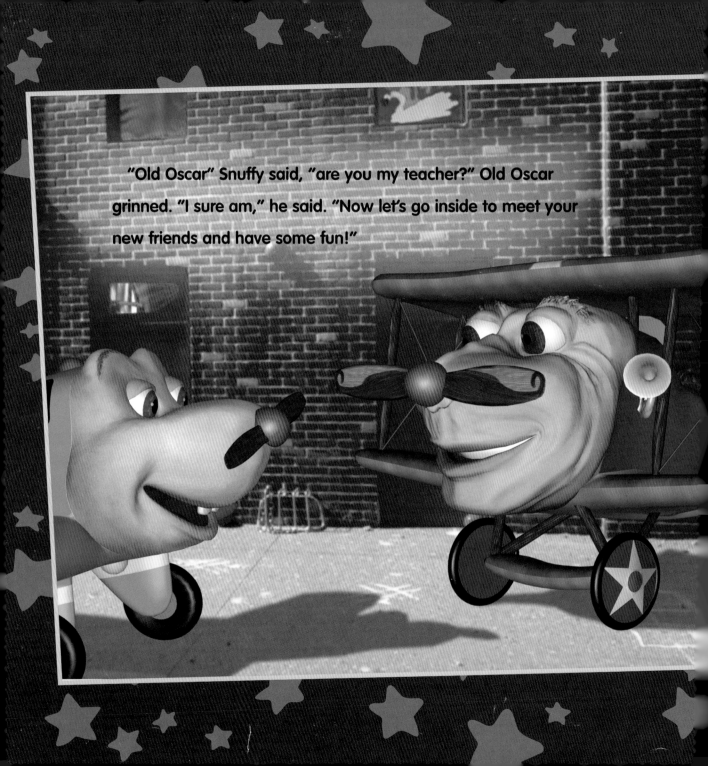

"Old Oscar" Snuffy said, "are you my teacher?" Old Oscar grinned. "I sure am," he said. "Now let's go inside to meet your new friends and have some fun!"